JONNY BRIGGS AND

"It's a good idea – making caves, isn't it?" said Jonny Briggs.

The class project on Stone Age life is greeted with enthusiasm and excitement, especially by Jonny.

When all his good ideas are sabotaged by the twins, he decides to build one of his own – in the best front-room!

JONNY BRIGGS
and the GIANT CAVE

Joan Eadington

Illustrated by William Marshall

as told in Jackanory by
Bernard Holley

BBC/KNIGHT

First published in Great Britain in 1982
by British Broadcasting Corporation/
Knight Books

Fourth impression 1989

British Library C.I.P.

Eadington, Joan
   Jonny Briggs and the Giant Cave –
   (Knight books)
I. Title   II. Marshall, William
823'.914[J]   PZ7

ISBN 0 340 38042 5
   (0 563 20034 0 BBC)

Printed and bound in Great Britain
for Hodder and Stoughton
Paperbacks, a division of Hodder and
Stoughton Ltd., Mill Road,
Dunton Green, Sevenoaks, Kent
TN13 2YA.
(Editorial Office: 47 Bedford Square,
London WC1B 3DP) by
Cox & Wyman Ltd., Reading

Contents

1
The Big Plan

Jonny Briggs was looking hard at Miss Broom. He was really *trying* to have a good day. His nose was shooting forward like an arrow and his eyes were glued to Miss Broom's piece of white chalk, as she wrote the name MISS MILLS in big, slow letters on the blackboard.

"Miss Mills is your new teacher until Easter," said Miss Broom – after she had told them all to sit up straight and pay attention about twenty times. "But don't think you're saying goodbye to me, because I shall be always somewhere near – to help Miss Mills. And I shall write down all the people who misbehave in my red notebook." And she looked very hard at Jonny. So hard that their eyes almost seemed to dance together.

Then Miss Broom went out of the classroom. As soon as she'd gone the place began to buzz like a bee-hive.

"They've got a new teacher in class three as well," said Peter, who sat next to Jonny. "And one in class two, upstairs. And they let you do all sorts of things! They let you measure the school and make telescopes. Some of them let you make anything you like!"

Jonny Briggs's heart leapt with joy. He liked making things, but he didn't seem to have made anything very much since his gold belt.

"Yes," said Pam sitting on top of her desk and bumping about excitedly so that her brown shiny hair bounced in its green ribbons. "They even built a house out of egg-boxes in class two, but Sylvia Spragg brought two boxes with eggs still in and they all fell on top of Sandy and he was all yellow and slimy."

Everyone started to laugh – then there was a big sh . . . sh . . . and scuffling as they got back in their seats when Miss Broom came back again with Miss Mills behind her.

At first Jonny could hardly believe it! Miss Mills was so *small*. She was almost the same size as he was, and she was wearing a pink dress and shoes with a criss-cross pattern on them. He liked her.

"They're all yours," said Miss Broom with a very strange smile as she went out of the room.

"What a bright-looking class," said Miss Mills cheerfully. "We are going to do a project. Our project is to find out what it was like living in the Stone Age. I was wondering if we could start by building caves. Either small caves – or one big cave . . . What do you think?"

A cave! There was a sudden silence. Nobody in the school had ever built a cave. Not even class six.

The Brown brothers were the first to recover. "Please miss – our uncle works in a quarry. He could drop off a load of rocks in the school yard."

"He could never," howled Josie, one of the twins. "Take no notice, miss. Their uncle lives in Australia!"

"A far better idea, miss," said her twin, Jinny, hastily swallowing a large orange fruit drop, "would be if we all went to visit some caves at the seaside instead . . . so as me and Josie can use our new torches . . ."

"Yes, yes . . .!" said everyone. And the twins looked all round the class and beamed – because for once they were popular with everyone, even Jonny Briggs.

"That's a very good idea, Jinny," said Miss Mills, "but if you did that you wouldn't be actually making a cave would you? We want to be able to make a cave

in this classroom. A cave big enough for a family to sit in and sleep in. But we can't use real stones. We'll need things like cardboard boxes and paper. So think about it and tell me some more ideas tomorrow. Now I think we'll do some reading until playtime." But Jonny couldn't help thinking about the cave, even when it was his turn to read.

He felt really excited as he ran home from school that day . . . how would *he*, Jonny Briggs, build a cave? He'd often made tents out of bed covers with Albert and Humph, but never a *cave*. So how would he do it?

He was pleased when he found he was the first one home. It meant he could sit about doing nothing and think, or just lie spread out on the floor reading a comic without someone like Rita tripping over him on purpose.

And as the kitchen clock ticked quietly, and Razzle gave him a friendly lick, he suddenly had an idea.

Why not make a cave at home right now? If he managed to do that, he'd be able to tell all the others how to make one when he got to school tomorrow.

But where to make it?

And then – like a flash of inspiration it came to him. In the front-room of course! Nobody ever went in the front-room – except when there was a party – or when Albert kept his bike there. But Albert's bike wasn't in the best front-room any longer. Only the other day mam had done a whirlwind clean of the best front-room ... and usually when she did a whirlwind clean – no one was allowed to go in and muck it up again for months and *months!* But making a cave in it wouldn't be mucking it up. He could start making it behind the armchair so that it was hidden a bit, then he could sort of drag one of the curtains over the top of it so that no one would catch sight of it if they popped their head round the door.

Quickly Jonny ran to mam's kitchen cupboard where she kept some old newspapers. His heart was beating a bit quicker. Speed was essential. He had to get all the things he needed for building his cave before anyone else got back, otherwise they'd be asking him why he was rooting about, and try to stop him. Then, marvel of marvels, he found two large cardboard grocery boxes stuck next to the

kitchen cabinet. One of them had an old torn table-cloth in it and it had pictures of *leaves* on it! Just like you might have leaves and twigs round the top of a cave . . . He could drape it all over the top of his cave! Maybe he could even paint it too, or stick some real old leaves on from dad's cabbage patch. Feverishly he carried the boxes and the cloth and the old news-papers to the front-room and hid them in a corner behind the chair near the window. It was a start. All he needed now was mam's clothes-airer that she used to hang the clothes on when she'd ironed them. She hardly ever used it.

It was a new one made of thin white metal bars like little ladders all folded together, and it was behind the door.

But no sooner had he lifted it out than the door slammed and in strolled Rita.

Jonny's hand shot away from the clothes-airer as if it were red hot and he felt himself shrinking as he heard Rita dump down all her sixth-form school books and say: "Home early eh? And just about to do something crafty – judging by the way you nearly jumped a mile when I came in! I hope you've not eaten all those chocolate biscuits."

"I didn't know we had any, our Rita. And why should you care: I thought you only lived on rabbit food and hot water!"

"You cheeky little . . .!" She suddenly looked at the space next to the kitchen cabinet where the card-board boxes had been: "Where've those boxes gone, our Jonny? There was a big tablecloth there. A special, very expensive, beautiful tablecloth. Mavis and I wanted that tablecloth. I was the one who rescued it from the dustbin. Mavis and I are going to share half each and go as Hula-Hula girls to this party in aid of the preservation of trees . . . That tablecloth with those pictures of leaves on it was ideal."

"What was that long word you said – before trees, our Rita?" said Jonny, trying to think of *anything* that would take Rita's mind off him and what he was doing.

"Tree *preservation*, our Jonny. Keeping trees preserved. Stopping them from being chopped down."

"I think that's a good idea, our Rita," said Jonny as he slipped quietly towards the back door and heard Rita still rabbiting on: "You see, Mavis and I have just met these two boys . . . well they're *men* actually and one's a . . ."

Taking Razzle's lead from the door, Jonny opened it and crept out into the yard. "Just taking Razzle for a walk to the park," he called.

And within ten minutes he was there. "I'll go back home again nearer teatime, when mam's back from work," he thought, "and by then, they'll all be so busy eating, no one'll want to know about boxes or anything else!"

It was nice in Albert Park. The grass was very green and great beds of tulips with green buds were standing in rows and rows by the sides of the smooth grey paths.

Then, as he walked towards the swings, he met Pam. "I've come out again," he said. "I'm going to try and make a cave later on."

"Make a cave?" her eyes widened. "Whereabouts?"

"In our best front-room behind the armchair. No one ever goes in."

"You lucky thing." She looked at him enviously and then patted Razzle: "I wish I could try making one. My mum won't even let our Stew wear his footy boots in *our* front-room. And she finds things straight away. I hid a packet of caramel fudge in a vase on the window ledge and she found it in five minutes. It's awful . . ."

They both looked very gloomy.

Then Jonny said: "It's a good idea – making caves though – isn't it . . .? If you can make them in the house. I thought I'd try and make this one and then I might creep down in the night and actually *sleep* in it . . ." He looked at her and drew a deep breath, then looked up at the sky and his breath came out all trembly with excitement.

"You lucky thing, Jonny Briggs," she said again. "I once went to see some caves at Margate when we visited my aunty. It was called the Shell Grotto, and you went down all these steps, and all the walls were decorated with sea-shells in all sorts of patterns. Some people said they'd been there for thousands of years – but other people said an old sailor did it all in his spare time. I wish we had a shell cave. . . ."

They both nodded and drew circles with their sandals on the ground – pushing bits of gravel away with their feet . . .

"P'raps we could get some shells," said Pam suddenly. "I could ask our dad to take us to Saltburn in the car to see Nana on Saturday. And I could ask him if you could come as well. There's a lot of shells and pebbles there. . . . Shall I ask him?"

Jonny nodded dumbly. A car trip to Saltburn! Nobody ever went on car trips to Saltburn in their family – leastways not him or Albert or Humph – or mam and dad. But with the girls it was different. They were always buzzing about with people who had cars. "Do you think your dad'll let us?" he said after a few seconds.

"He might . . . if he's in a good temper. I'll let you know at school tomorrow. And I'll bring the book all about the Shell Grotto to show Miss Mills."

As they waved goodbye, Jonny felt really happy again. He felt full of energy as if he could build the cave in the front-room in the twinkle of an eye – as if it would be as easy as wink – as simple as a smile – no problems . . . And he smiled as he saw himself creeping out of bed later that night – away from Albert's sharp toe-nails – down into his own special sleeping quarters complete with Humph's sleeping bag and two packets of cheese and onion crisps and a bottle of water in case of emergency.

"Wherever have you been?" said mam when he arrived back. "I was going to send someone out to

look for you! We've all had our tea ages ago. And get
that filthy face washed. And just *look* at that shirt.
And get those shoes off – they're caked with mud and
it stinks!"

Jonny sighed. Mam was in one of her tetchy
moods. She was rushing round and scowling.

"I've only been in the park, our mam."

"Only been in the park?" hooted Albert whose
ears were flapping like a flying elephant as he hastily
scraped the last remnants of a jug of custard before
Jonny could get any. "He looks as if he's come out of a
swamp doesn't he mam? He looks like a cave-man!"

"Cave?" Jonny echoed the word. He looked startled as Albert grinned at him wickedly from beneath his dark floppy hair. Jonny's heart jumped slightly. Did Albert know anything about his cave plans . . .? No . . . how could he?

"His class are going to build caves, our mam," said Albert. "Archy Brown's two kid brothers were full of it."

"Build caves?" said mam, looking alarmed. "That doesn't sound very safe. Are you sure, Albert?"

"Positive."

"They've got this new teacher and she asked Archy Brown's lot to get their uncle to deliver a whole load of stones to the school yard to build caves with."

"She never did!" said Jonny, going scarlet.

"The things they get up to in schools these days!"

"But it's not true, mam! It's not like that. Albert's got it all wrong . . ."

"When I was at school we never built caves."

"Because you *lived* in them then, didn't you mam?" called Albert cheerfully as he galloped out of the room. "And maybe our Pat'll have to live in one when she and Dale get married. . . ."

"Married! Is our Pat getting married, mam?" asked Jonny as she dished him out some baked beans and chips.

"It seems like it," sighed mam, as if she didn't want to talk about it. "Goodness knows what your dad'll say. She and Dale are far too young . . ." Then, as if to change the subject, she said: "Now look here

Jonny. Just you be careful about all this cave build-ing. And I mean it. Caves are dangerous places. You must *never* go in caves alone or with other children. You could be trapped or killed. It's all very well reading exciting tales about them, but that's not real life. In *real* life. . . ."

"I *know*, mam . . . Albert's got it wrong. Why do you always believe him and not me? We're just going to make some *models* of caves in the classroom, that's all. So we can imagine what it was like in the Stone Age. It's very *interesting*. . . ."

"Interesting?" His mother stopped rushing about and suddenly smiled. "Interesting, son? That's the first time I've ever heard you use that word! Fancy . . ."

Then she began to clear the table and wash the pots, and Jonny finished his tea on his own. He'd build the greatest cave ever . . . and even sleep in it. And tell Miss Mills all about it at school tomorrow.

And as he finally wiped round his plate with a piece of bread-and-butter he began to work out where everyone in the house was, so that he could build his cave all undisturbed.

And this is how it was.

Mam – kitchen. Busy washing-up, then out to visit her friend Madge in Middlesbrough General Hospital.

Albert – upstairs with a bit of the bed wedged against the bedroom door to keep everyone else out whilst he read a book about gliders. Then out to see his latest pal – Tommy Wilton.

Humph – not yet in at all because he was out playing cricket.

Pat – gone straight on from working at the chemist's to do ice-skating at Billingham Forum.

Sandra – gone round to Marilyn's.

Rita – Jonny sniffed nervously – out at last. Round at Mavis's house telling her about the missing table-cloth.

And dad – out doing something at the Works Social Club.

Paradise! Peace at last.

Quickly, Jonny slipped like an almost invisible shadow to the quiet, peaceful secrecy of the best front-room and began work. . . .

2
Late For School

Jonny Briggs had made it!

He felt like running to the old record player and putting on mam's favourite record very loud. It was called *I Did It My Way*. But he knew that if he did, the whole house would leap out of bed in a panic. Because he was – at this very minute – in his own cave in the middle of the night, with the rest of the family upstairs snoring their heads off.

Yes, he, Jonny Briggs, was crouched on a cushion behind the armchair in the front-room, with the metal clothes-airer surrounding him. Albert's cycle lamp cast mysterious glowing lights on the tablecloth spread across the cave top, which was covered with cabbage leaves and scraps of grass from the yard. The sides were big brown rocky boulders – all knobbly looking – made out of cardboard grocery boxes, and newspapers guarded the entrance to the cave.

Jonny yawned happily. Beside him was the solitary remaining piece of a dead Stone Age wild animal (a sheep's head painted blue which Humph had once found on the Yorkshire moors and usually kept hidden in a drawer). There was an old bone of Razzle's as well. It was just like a *real* Stone Age cave . . . just wait till he told them all. . . .

He nibbled one or two salted peanuts resting on a blackish lump of slate which had once blown off a roof in Port Street, and began to doze a bit. Finished at last, he thought. His own cave, without a single interruption. And the clock in the living-room showing it was three o'clock in the morning! Jonny shivered, half from happiness and half from leaving a warm bed upstairs. It had been very hard – planning to wake up in the middle of the night to come down here. But he'd managed it because he'd banged his head twice on the pillow before he fell asleep which meant *wake at two* . . . it had all worked out.

And with that he gave a big smile and promptly fell asleep, flopping back in bliss onto the newspaper and bone-strewn floor of his cave.

"T . . r . . r . . r . ." The alarm clock was ringing in mam and dad's bedroom.

"Half-past six," growled dad, as he gave it a smart bang with a heavy fist and went back to sleep for another ten minutes. Mam tipped out of bed, struggled into Rita's old fluffy purple slippers with the fluff hanging off, and creaked downstairs to put the kettle on.

Then she took dad a cup of tea and popped into the boys' room to give them their first nudge of the morning. Mam reckoned that it took at least three quiet reminders, two yells, a bellow, and even a wet cloth round the ears before any of them stirred.

And then . . . her face fell a mile and she went quite

weak at the knees. She clutched her blue-striped nightie and stared at the bed usually occupied by Humph, Albert and Jonny. For all she could see now was Humph at one side, a big gap, and then Albert at the other side.

She looked in the bathroom, then went back to her own bedroom and started rattling about in the dressing-table drawer.

"What on earth's up?" said dad as he sipped his tea.

"I'm looking for those strong glasses, love – the ones Aunty Aida once left," said mam. "My eyes aren't what they were. I couldn't see our Jonny in bed this morning."

"I'm not surprised," said dad. "He's probably been squashed out of existence. We'll have to do something about it. I was thinking that if I got a bit of wood I could make bunk beds for two of 'em and there'd be room for one single. Bunk beds would be the answer in that room. I know a fellow who could get some off-cuts . . ."

"But he's not squashed in the bed! It was flat. Come and have a look."

Reluctantly, dad followed her to the boys' room. They both went over to the bed and stared at it.

Albert and Humph were still dead to the world. Humph's monkey face was quite smooth and Albert had his mouth wide open and it was making a feather wobble on top of the eiderdown.

"Have you looked underneath?" dad said. "Don't

ask me to bend down with *my* back or I'll never be able to get up again."

Mam bent down and peered under the bed, wincing as she saw mountains of cloudy fluff mixed with tattered grey canvas P.E. shoes and down-at-heel track shoes with laces missing.

"Not a sign of him . . ."

"He must be downstairs then," muttered dad irritably. "What about breakfast? He's probably out jogging. It's a free world you know." Then he stamped down to the kitchen to get a shave.

Mam sighed and followed him to start getting out the cornflakes. "Boys like Jonny don't go jogging. It's only people like Mr Prince across the road who do that sort of thing!" And she became so worried she put a lemon in dad's bait box instead of an orange. "Supposing he's been kidnapped?"

"Kidnapped – talk sense, woman! How could he be kidnapped?" Dad began to hack the rind off his bacon because he hated all this fuss. "Look: did you see him go to bed last night?"

"Yes, but . . ."

"But what then? He must have got up early, that's all. He'll have taken Razzle for a walk . . ."

But when dad went out in the yard to check up, Razzle was sleeping peacefully in his kennel. The lines on dad's face went deeper as he got ready to set off for work. "If you really get worried," he called, "you know where to get in touch. Just ring Jack on extension 757."

"Whatever's been going on, our mam?" said Rita when she and the others were up at last. "It's been awful lying there listening to you prowling about everywhere. What've you lost?"

"Our Jonny," mumbled mam shamefacedly. "And it's time for me to be out. I'll just have to tell them at the shop – and come back here to see if he's back. Then if he isn't I shall go to the police."

"The police'll be right fed up with us," said Albert, inking in a hole in the back of his sock with a ball point pen. "They never got over the time he was out ghost-hunting."

"He's nothing but trouble," said Rita, standing at

the mirror putting eye-liner on. "I blame him for losing that expensive material belonging to Mavis and me. It means that we might have to go to that party in our ordinary clothes because of him! He kills everything."

Mam sighed, then she said: "Talking of material, tell our Pat not to forget to bring back the stuff for the bridesmaids' dresses. It's going to take quite a long time machining wedding outfits for her and four bridesmaids." Then sadly muttering, ". . . they don't know what they're letting themselves in for . . ." mam dashed out to work.

The rest of them were rather quiet after that, and Sandra and Pat went out with hardly a word. For to tell the truth they were all feeling worried. It just wasn't like Jonny not to be around at breakfast time. It left a sort of gap. It didn't somehow seem as lively. Even Albert drifted down the street extra slowly as Rita hobbled past him in her high-heeled sandals.

There was only Humph left now in the house . . . or so it seemed. Humph catching up on his physics homework – he was going to school later because of a dental appointment.

Humph frowned to himself . . . very strange about their Jonny . . . very strange indeed. Usually he was buzzing about feeding Razzle and playing with him – but today Razzle had been ignored completely.

Humph went to the back door and opened it and immediately Razzle came bounding in, wagging his tail and sniffing about all round the kitchen. Humph found him some crunchy biscuits and a drink of water.

Then Razzle did a strange thing. Instead of waiting for his food he began to sniff and whimper at the living-room door. And when Humph opened it he went to the door leading to the hall and began to sniff and whimper at that . . . until finally he was standing sniffing and whimpering and giving short excited barks at the closed door of the best front-room.

"Whatever's got into you?" said Humph, opening the door in exasperation and watching Razzle leap with joy towards the window where the armchair was. The next minute he knew – because Razzle was back again beside him with a large bone in his mouth, wagging his tail.

"So *that* was it . . ." smiled Humph. He stood stock still as he heard a creaking and a rustling coming from the corner.

"That you Humph? What time is it?"

"Jonny!" Humph jumped across to the chair and peered at the cave behind it. "Gordon Highlanders! What the hell are you doing? The place's been in an uproar. Mam's nearly off her rocker."

"Where is she . . .?" said Jonny, suddenly coming to. He realised all was not well.

"Gone to work of course. So you'd better beat it to school before she's back again. She's only gone to ask them for some time off so as she can hunt round for you. She'll do her *nut!*"

Hurriedly Jonny scrambled out of the cave. Nearly nine o'clock! He'd be late for school. There was nothing worse to start the day than being late for school!

Mr Badger was terrible when you were late for school. He made you stand in the corridor while everyone else sang hymns in the hall, then all the rest of the school walked past you and stared. After that Mr Badger made you walk into the empty hall and tell him why you were late, and if you hadn't got a good enough excuse you had to stay in at play-time. Jonny hated that. Playtime was the best part of school.

"Hurry up and get those cornflakes down you," said Humph as he ran a comb through Jonny's hair and even found his shoes for him. "And don't worry about mam. I'll think of something to soothe her with. I'll leave her a note if she's not back by the time I go to the dentist's."

31

As Jonny scrambled off down Port Street towards school, he began to hope and pray that he might just manage to get there in time – but as he arrived at the school yard his hopes fell, for he could see all the mothers strolling away from the large metal gates. Inside it was flat and grey and silent, and he could see the heads of children bobbing about through the classroom windows. They must have already been in the hall, which meant that he was extra, *terribly* late.

His stomach went all crampy and he began to wonder whether it was worth going in at all! He turned towards the gates again . . . Nadine's brother worked on a furniture delivery van before he was on the dole . . . P'raps he should go to the town and see if *he* could get a delivery van job. Perhaps mam'd let him keep it – if he got one and he was paid. But he knew – in his heart of hearts – she wouldn't, and he remembered – in his ear of ears – their Rita once going on about it being against the law to work when you were young like him. . . .

Then he remembered the cave. . . . What about telling Miss Mills about how he'd managed to build it? And what about Pam and the others?

Almost trembling, he turned back again and stole inside to the warmth and gentle hum of noise and activity – with every so often a loud ear-splitting roar from class five where Mr Hobbs was. And as he tried to walk extra smartly down the corridor – as if he wasn't late at all – he hoped and prayed that he wouldn't meet Mr Badger.

He had almost reached his classroom, when he heard someone call him. "Jonny Briggs . . ." His heart froze.

It was Miss Broom. "Come here and take these books to Miss Mills for me."

Eagerly he went towards her: "Yes miss."

Miss Broom handed him three big books with pictures of cave men on them. "Tell her it's all I could find."

"Yes miss."

"Yes Miss *Broom*, Jonny."

"Yes miss!" said Jonny enthusiastically. He went towards the classroom again, clutching the books, and opened the door.

Miss Mills was sitting at her desk checking some money and before she could speak, Jonny said:

"Please Miss Mills, Miss Broom sent you these three books. They were all she could find. She asked me to bring them." Then he sat down quickly.

"Please miss, he's *late*," said Josie quickly, putting out her tongue at him.

"Yes, miss . . ." said Jinny getting up and going to the table at the front of the class. "You're supposed to get sent to Mr Badger if you're late . . ."

"Please miss," said Jonny quickly, "I–I've made the cave miss. . . . The cave like you told us yesterday."

"Take no notice – he's a liar, miss," said Jinny, poking her face right into Miss Mills's face and rolling her eyes.

Miss Mills looked at Jinny, then she said: "Excuse me . . . but which class are you in?"

"This one . . . miss."

"Then sit down please, like all the rest."

Jinny sat down, scowling, and Miss Mills looked in her register and put a tick next to Jonny Briggs's name. Then she smiled and said: "Thank you for the books, Jonny. Now tell us all about the cave. . . ."

And so he told them all . . . and even about how he fell asleep in it and didn't know how late it was.

"I was nearly late for school," he said breathlessly at the end.

"NEARLY?" shouted the twins again. "He *was* late, miss. It isn't fair!" But their voices were drowned by all the people wanting to talk about Stone Age caves, and Jonny knew he was safe at last.

Later on at playtime, Pam said: "I asked dad about going to Saltburn in the car to look for shells and things and he says you can come. It'll be Saturday afternoon. Be at our house at two o'clock and put your wellies on."

Jonny nodded. "Should I put my gold belt on an' all?"

"Yes, put it on, then our dad can see it."

"Yippeee!" said Jonny, suddenly leaping into the air. "See you on Saturday then," and he began to run headlong all round the school yard.

When school ended that day he felt as if he was walking on air. Everything had turned out right, and Miss Mills had even drawn his cave on the board and chalked in the cabbage leaves on top. Everyone had crowded round Jonny and asked him if he could get them some cabbage leaves. He positively burst into the house when he got back – he was so full of happiness.

But as he burst in – something large blocked his way. It was mam . . . in her Millicent of the Yard mood. She gripped him hard on the shoulders: "Whoa there, son. So what do you think you've been up to, eh? What was this note I found from Humph – saying you'd got up in the night and fallen asleep in a corner? I don't believe a word of it! Do you realise I've been worried sick and missed nearly all today off work? I've a good mind to tan your backside so hard you won't be able to sit down for a week! Our Rita's quite right. You do nothing but cause trouble. Trouble, *trouble*, TROUBLE!" She shook him hard.

Jonny went pale. There was no one else in yet. He went up to the bedroom and lay on the bed. Don't say they were all going to get at him about it at teatime. Don't say that!

He lay there not even daring to read a comic. He was all tense and miserable. What was the best thing to make it all blow over and bring mam into a better mood?

He began to wonder about his cave in the front-room. Was it still there? Mam hadn't mentioned that . . . falling asleep in a corner, was all she'd mentioned. But he didn't dare to go in the front-room to look. . . .

Slowly he got off the bed again and wandered silently into mam and dad's bedroom and looked through the window down to Port Street. Any minute now they would all be coming in.

He groaned as he saw Rita just turning the corner, still hobbling in her high heels and carrying her school books. Then he saw Albert appear with a bunch of other boys as they occasionally tripped each other up or chased someone across the road in a mad scurry. Not Albert *and* Rita in first, not *that!*

Then suddenly his heart leapt up as a small battered car came churning down the street and stopped outside his own front door. And he saw dad get out. Then he saw dad take a whole load of bits of wood from the boot and wave to Jack Stubbs who sometimes gave him a lift to work. Then he heard dad come in and shout: "I've got some. I'll start tonight."

Jonny's heart leapt. Thank goodness for dad!

He ran downstairs eagerly – to see what it was all about.

3
Tipped Out

"Yes, I know it's a very good idea – getting some wood to make them," said mam as she dumped the food down in front of everyone. "Yes – dad – I never said they weren't a good idea. I'm very pleased . . ."

But Jonny didn't think she looked a bit pleased.

Then she glared at Humph and said: "Yes, Humph, I agree that three in a bed is too much. But I do *not* believe that half the time you sleep on the floor in your sleeping-bag."

Humph's monkey face crinkled up. He didn't say any more but Jonny knew that sometimes he did sleep on the floor – but he always said it was practising for camping.

Then mam muttered: "Why oh why does everyone start saying all this at teatime?" And she slammed down Rita's fruit pie so hard that the plate cracked. It was an old plate – but all the same there was an awful silence, and even Rita looked slightly shocked as she lifted up the pie and delicately laid it on the tablecloth. Then she put the cracked plate into the wastebin with a wounded expression on her face, and proceeded to give mam a lecture: "That plate was already cracked a bit, our mam. You should never use cracked plates or chipped cups! There's millions of germs lives in all those little rough bits. They can live there for years – spreading diseases. No wonder I've had so many colds this year . . . it's probably because – "

"Shut up – miss . . ." said dad, scowling quietly. Then he said to mam: "What the heck's got into you love?"

"It's you lot that's got into me," said mam. "First our Jonny disappearing in the night – right on top of our Pat announcing her marriage to the world and wanting me to be the sewing machine skivvy . . ."

"Mam, what a *horrible* thing to say about a wedding!" cried Pat as a large piece of apple almost fell from her mouth. "You *love* making things on the sewing machine! What about all my ice-skating skirts? You should be *proud* that I'm letting you make all the dresses . . ."

Then she got up from the table and rushed upstairs to have a good weep. Jonny heard her go to the bathroom and douse her face in cold water like she always did – before she came down again to ask if there was any more pie left.

"I thought you liked weddings, our mam," said Albert. "When Enid Prince got married you said there was nothing like a good wedding to brighten things up."

"As long as it's not mine and Dale's," said Pat, glaring.

Jonny said nothing. Nobody was noticing him at all, and he felt quite peaceful. He looked at dad who was busy working out some measurements on a scrap of paper while he drank his mug of tea. Jonny was glad Pat was getting married. Then she could become a world ice-skating champion with Dale and go and practise in another country and leave more space in the bathroom. And his heart glowed happily as he imagined Rita married as well. Rita telling everyone she was going to live far away in a deep forest helping to look after trees.

"Well, mam, there's one thing for sure – I don't intend to get married for years and years." It was Rita's voice. "In fact Mavis and I might not even get married at all. Mavis and I are quite happy as we are."

"About this wood for the bunks . . ." said dad.

"There's no need for any excitement. I'll get out of the way and saw it up in the front-room."

"The front-room?" Mam's face went quite wild looking. "I'm not having that sort of thing going on. I shall need that front-room to do the machining in, for all the wedding dresses. The girls and I will need that front-room – "

Dad sighed, and tapped his pencil on the table as if he were trying very hard to stay patient: "Look – if I can't make these bunks in the front-room where can I make 'em? The out-house isn't big enough and it's full of mop-buckets and old brushes and paint tins! These bunk beds'll only take me a couple of days, then you can have the front-room for ever . . ."

Jonny watched mam's face anxiously. All the time at the back of his mind was the thought of his cave in the front-room. Was it still there? If dad went in the front-room with his wood would he see the cave? Perhaps if dad, alone, knew all about it he'd even let the cave *stay* there . . .

But if mam knew . . . if the girls knew. . . . Jonny shivered slightly, not knowing whether the females of the family had already tipped out the cave without saying anything. He just hadn't dared to go in and look since he crept out of it earlier that morning.

At last mam seemed to give in and relax. She sat down opposite dad at the table, poured herself a cup of tea and began to eat her own fruit pie: "All right then," she said, "two days and that's all. After that, it's for me and the girls."

"Shall I help you to carry the wood in from the hall, dad?" said Jonny, smiling with relief.

"Righto son – but mind you don't bash it against anything otherwise our lives won't be worth living." And he nodded, and gave Jonny a slight wink.

Carefully, Jonny took one of the pieces of wood and struggled with it into the front-room – laying it flat on the floor between some chairs – then quickly he glanced towards the window. Yes, his cave was there. Completely untouched! He stood over it. It was just like a real cave – with all those cabbage leaves on top and the skull inside . . . "I wish I could live in it during the day . . ." he thought. "I wish I could come home from school and have my tea in it. And have meals in it at weekends . . . I wish it could stay there for *ever*."

Then dad came in. He looked at the wood on the floor: "We can't leave it there, Jonny. We'll have to clear some of the stuff out of here for a while. We'll have to get rid of all these ornaments and the chairs and bring in that small kitchen table to work on. And we'll have to roll up this bit of carpet and put it in the hall for a while."

Then he walked over to the window, looked down at Jonny's cave and said: "What on earth's that? Is it a cave or summat?"

"It's a *Stone Age cave*, dad," Jonny answered quickly, so that dad would know it was something special.

"Stone Age cave with my cabbage leaves on?" said dad doubtfully. "Was that where you were then, in the night?"

Jonny nodded: "I fell asleep." Then he added: "Miss Mills at school wants us to build one in the classroom."

"So you can *all* fall asleep in it while she sits there eating a box of chocolates all to herself?" joked dad, and his eyes began to sparkle a bit. "The last time I was crouched in anything like a cave, son, was in the war in one of those tin shelters. And may it never happen to you."

Jonny nodded: "Were you allowed to live in it and have meals in it?"

"We weren't *allowed* to, we were FORCED to! It was in next door's garden, all soaking wet and muddy and horrible. And we ate cakes like lead weights made from potatoes instead of flour. That sort of cooking wouldn't have suited our Sandra one tiny bit."

"I'd have liked it," Jonny said. "I'd like to stay in here in this room in this cave and have all my meals in it."

Dad grunted and shook his head. Then he said: "Keep your cave then, if you want, but help me to get the rest of the stuff out of the way and let's get these bunks made before you lads grow another six feet." Then, as Jonny helped him to move things and helped him with measuring the wood, and held it steady, Jonny told dad about how Pam said he could go to Saltburn-by-the-sea on Saturday, to get pebbles and shells, and how he was going to wear his gold belt. And dad seemed very pleased and patted Jonny's head and even felt in his trouser pocket and produced a fifty-pence piece for Jonny to take with him . . .

That night, at supper-time, when mam had given Jonny his cup of cocoa and some bread and he'd gone off to bed and she and dad were all quiet and peaceful again, she said: "Now would you credit it! He's up there in his bed – safe and sound and fast asleep – but now my cup and plate are missing. If there's one thing I can't stand it's suddenly coming across an empty cocoa cup growing fur inside it a year later. Has he left it in that front-room along with the plate?"

Dad jumped up from his chair like a Jack-in-a-box. "Our Jonny's cup . . .? Front-room . . . Err . . . Don't worry love. Just sit there and rest . . . I'll see to it." And before mam could move he was back with the cup and plate.

"Where were they then?" said mam.

"In the ca . . ." Dad stopped suddenly.

"In the what?" asked mam suspiciously, but dad was already pretending not to hear as he buried himself back behind the *Evening Gazette*.

"Mixed in the curtains, no doubt, or lying in mountains of chippings and chisels and chunks of wood, I suppose," she said, as she took the pots away.

Dad took out his handkerchief and patted his brow. "Phew . . ." he muttered. "Phew. . . ."

At two o'clock on Saturday afternoon Jonny Briggs, with his jeans tucked in his wellies and wearing a new anorak and his gold belt, arrived at Pam's to go to Saltburn-by-the-sea. He was carrying a plastic bucket.

"My dad's in a very *good* temper, and he's got his new knitted jersey on. It's because he saw our Stew's

name mentioned in a sports report." Pam showed
Jonny the goldfish pond in the back garden while Mr
Dean got the car out. Then Mrs Dean, who had dark
hair and a fringe, came out of the back door and gave
Pam a cake to take to her Nana and told them both to
be careful on the cliffs but to have a good time.

"Before we all visit Nana," said Mr Dean, "I'll just
pop down to see Ian in the Smuggler's while you two
get all those shells and things from the beach."

The road to the Smuggler's Inn was very steep and
winding but there was a flat silvery car-park at the
bottom where Mr Dean parked his car.

He took Pam and Jonny to the Smuggler's Inn
across the gush of water which came from the stream
near the Italian Gardens, and pointed to the wooden
chairs and tables outside the Inn.

"When you're finished, wait there for me, then we'll walk along the path by the miniature railway and climb up through the wood to the house where Nana lives."

Jonny was really excited. The sun shone in a fresh blue sky and the smooth wet sand was like deep honey fudge as he and Pam put shells into one plastic bucket, and bluey-grey pebbles into another.

"I'll bet our cave'll be the best in the class," Johnny shouted triumphantly as the sea sparkled and the sea-gulls sang.

Then his happiness came zooming to the ground like a crashed plane as Pam said in a puzzled voice: "It can't be the best in the class Jonny, because there's only going to be one cave. Didn't you hear Miss Mills say? She said it again on Friday afternoon just before we were going home. She said it would be best if we all got together and made one GIANT CAVE. . . ."

Jonny stopped dead: "Giant Cave? All of us – all the class? I never heard her! I thought some were doing a big cave and people like you and me could do our own?"

"It was when you were out with Peter washing all the paint pots. She said we can all do different parts of the Giant Cave. You and me are putting pebbles round the door and sticking shells on the walls and the twins are – "

"THE TWINS?" Jonny's nose wrinkled with almost tearful disgust and disappointment. "I'm not making a cave with *them!* They'll wreck everything!"

"But she said we've all got to share the work. It's *everyone*'s cave . . . Nadine's bringing a real goatskin rug for it, and Lily Spencer's cutting out a bright red pool of blood from a picture in an old nursing book of her mother's. She says they had lots of pools of blood in the Stone Age. And the Brown brothers are . . . Jonny, aren't you listening?"

Jonny blinked sadly. Suddenly all the fun had vanished. So it wasn't going to be just him and Pam after all. It was going to be *everyone*. Everyone fighting and squabbling and him getting blamed all the time – because, make no mistake, if those twins were anywhere around they always squabbled and blamed Jonny Briggs!

"Cheer up," said Pam. "It'll be even better if we all do some. It really will be a giant cave. And the twins might be quite . . ."

"Might be quite HORRIBLE," said Jonny in a loud voice. "I'll bet they'll pull all the shells off the minute we've stuck them on! I'll bet they'll poke holes in the walls with their pencils and pinch the pebbles to put on their path at home! I'll bet. . . ."

But he never finished because Mr Dean arrived and soon they were on their way to see Pam's Nana.

"The house where she lives is supposed to have a secret passage," said Mr Dean. "It was once an old rectory and there was a passage right up from the Smuggler's Inn where smugglers brought stuff in by boat at night-time hundreds of years ago."

But even the thought of that couldn't cheer up Jonny as they finally arrived at the large, sandy yellow house standing in a big garden.

Then Jonny saw lots of other people too, and one looked a bit like his own Grandad.

"They're special flats, specially for Nanas and Grandads," said Pam, as she led Jonny to a door inside with "Mrs Green" written on it.

"How nice to see you all!" said Mrs Green. "And thanks for the cake. Let's all have some right now and I'll put the kettle on."

Jonny liked her. She had very white hair and wore a pale blue dress with fancy buttons on it. And she had two gold rings on her fingers. He opened his anorak a bit so as to show off his gold belt. And she noticed straight away!

"What a nice belt," she said. Then Jonny and Pam told her all about how it was made. Then they told her about making the giant cave at school.

"But Jonny's frightened the twins'll wreck it and blame us . . ." said Pam.

Her Nana looked very thoughtful, then she said: "The thing to do will be to keep those twins so busy while you're building the giant cave that they won't have time to pull off the shells or poke holes in it. You'll just have to think up a way to keep them occupied. I'm sure you'll manage it. I wouldn't let a set of twins ruin *my* cave!"

On the way back to Middlesbrough with their pebbles and shells, Jonny said: "I like your Nana. We must stop the twins from wrecking things, so that it's a real giant Stone Age cave. P'raps Miss Mills'll let us drink our milk in it when it's finished – or take it in turns to guard it . . ."

As he walked back from Pam's to his own home in Port Street, his spirits rose. Yes – a giant cave would be really good. Miss Mills might let them use the school ladders. It might be such a giant cave that it would nearly reach the classroom ceiling . . . they could even make the whole *classroom* into one . . . they could cover up all the windows with black paper and move the desks into the hall and he could bring Razzle to guard it all. . . . Mmmmm, he suddenly saw Mr Badger's face in a large balloon in his mind's eye. No – perhaps that would be *too* big. . . . Anyway he did have his very own special cave, in the front-room at home. He began to skip as he went round to the back yard door. Then he stopped . . .

Cautiously he opened the kitchen door. As soon as he set foot inside, he knew everything was different. Pleasantly different. It even smelt different. It smelt new . . . like new clothes.

Everyone had finished their tea ages ago. All the pots were washed and the place was as neat as a new pin in the warm spring-like evening. He heard voices calling and chattering and doors opening and closing – and even people laughing . . .

The door of the kitchen swung wide open and dad came through – his shirt collar loose and his face sweating slightly, but as bright and shining as the day when he said he and the lads at work had got four correct away matches on the football pools.

"The bunks are finished, son," he said. "You'll be sleeping like royalty tonight . . . our Jonny . . . Just like royalty. . . ."

4
The New Life

Jonny could hardly believe his ears about the bunks. "But how could you have finished them so quickly, dad?"

"Help, son. Humph and Albert helped, and Joe called round and all. They worked like Trojans."

"What's Trojans?" said Jonny, just as Humph came into the kitchen.

"Trojans," said dad, "are people who work hard."

Humph said: "Trojans are a group of asteroids, our Jonny — and they perform complicated oscillations — so it amounts to the same thing . . ."

Then Jonny said: "I know the bunks'll be very nice an' all — and I know our Albert won't be stabbing me with his toe-nails any more . . . but won't it be a bit hard, just lying on wood, dad?" Then he added bravely: "But lying on wood does keep your back straight doesn't it dad? And Aunty Betty once had to lie on a board when she had a slipped disc, didn't she? So it must be good for you in the end."

"Mattresses, son . . ." said dad, patting him gently on the shoulder.

"We got three mattresses this afternoon," said Humph with quiet satisfaction. "Three journeys from the town *and* we carried 'em!"

"But what about our old bed?" gasped Jonny.

"A present to our Marilyn. They came over and shifted it this afternoon to their spare room."

Jonny's lip quivered very slightly. It was all such a shock! "I hope the comics haven't – "

"Fear not," said Humph. "Even Ice Man himself is still there at the bottom of the pile. But watch out, our Jonny, there's even more of a change going on downstairs, isn't there dad?"

Dad nodded slowly: "That's why I'm off in a few minutes to have a couple of games of bowls," he said.

Nervously, Jonny opened the door leading into the living-room and as he did so he heard Rita laying down the law to Mavis about whether Pat should have a white wedding in a church and whether dad would be able to afford a proper "do" or whether it would just be a cup of tea and an arrowroot biscuit. Mavis was crawling about the floor picking up pins under the table. And, on top of the table in front of Rita and a large pair of orange-handled scissors, lay the tablecloth.

"Where's our mam, Rita?" he said, trying not to look at any of it, and praying there wouldn't be a sudden explosion.

"Oh, so *you're* back are you?" said Rita. "And how, may I ask, did *my* special dress material with the leaves on land on your silly little cave in the front-room? Mavis and I found it just in the nick of time. But it means we're having to work like the clappers, doesn't it Mavis?" She bent down rather lazily to see how Mavis was going on with the pins. "*And* we've had to wash it all and get it dried and ironed so as to go as Hula-Hula girls tonight. *And* we may even have to finish up fastening them on with safety-pins . . ."

Then – to Jonny's relief they seemed to forget him completely as they started to take off half their clothes and drape the bits of tablecloth round each other, with Mavis saying: "A wire bracelet's what you need, Rita . . . just to set it off. I'll bring one along to the dance tonight made of a strand from that bit of wire cable those electricity men once gave us . . ."

And Rita said: "I seem to have *expanded* round my bust, Mavis. I'm not sure whether that's a good thing . . . or a bad thing. . . ."

Quietly, Jonny closed the door behind him and went into the front-room at last. He could hear mam's voice talking, and things smelt even newer . . . He could even hear the whirr of the sewing machine.

From wood . . . to weddings . . . all in a couple of hours! Sometimes life seemed really fast. Other times it was slow for ages and ages.

The room was completely transformed! It was covered with great mountains of silky dress material. And as he stood there he glanced quickly towards the window to see if any of his cave was still left, but there wasn't a sign . . .

"Either come right in or stay out," said mam cheerfully as she licked a silky strand of cotton and then threaded it carefully through the gleaming little needle on the sewing machine. "But if you do come in – don't go whisking about. We don't want dust blowing everywhere. And mind you don't tread on that paper pattern or disturb that piece of white velvet."

Jonny stood and gaped. Nothing like this had ever happened in his life before.

Oh yes, quite often mam machined bits of things for the girls, and once she even made him a shirt out of Humph's old one. Even Sandra made herself a dress from time to time. But never had Jonny seen the

front-room covered with blue silky stuff and milky cream velvet. And paper patterns with funny marks and writing on them all spread about. And their Pat leaning against the window-ledge writing an invitation list while Sandra tacked bits of cloth together with big white stitches.

"Is the wedding next week, mam?" said Jonny in a cautious daze. . . . Because now he didn't quite know where he was!

"No, son. Not for another three months. But we haven't got all day and every day to do the work. So we'll just have to work at it in the front-room. Just remember that from now on *nothing* has to be touched or taken out of here."

"Will I be going to the wedding, mam?"

"Of course you will, Jonny. What a daft thing to say! All of you will."

"Shall I wear my gold belt . . . with it all being special . . .?"

Mam hesitated. But in a flash Pat said: "Certainly not! We can't have him in that gold belt. It'll clash with everything. You'll just have to buy him a neat two-piece suit, mam, and let him sit near the door of the church with Albert and collect the hymn books when it's all over . . ."

Jonny's face fell, but Sandra smiled and said: "If I ever get married, Jonny, we'll all wear gold belts."

Pat glared at her.

"Did you have a nice time at Saltburn then?" asked mam.

He nodded.

"Have you been upstairs yet to look in the bedroom?"

Slowly he shook his head: "No but I'll go now . . ."

Then, closing the door behind him and glad to escape because it all seemed so strange and overwhelming, he ran upstairs away from it, to the peace and safety of the empty bedroom.

He stopped.

Dare he open the door? What would he find? Would there really be new beds inside? He could never remember any new beds in the house ever before. He could remember a cot which must have been his – years and years ago which got given to the bin-men . . . but new beds. . . . Never!

Gently, he turned the handle of the door and pushed it – letting the door swing open on its own, and his face glowed.

It was true! There in the room with its faded, rather grubby-looking, wallpaper were three bright, new, separate beds: one on its own and two built one on top of the other.

On the single bed was Humph's book on Astronomy and his belongings in a hurried, untidy pile.

On the bottom bunk were all Albert's things in a hurried heap with a big card on top saying MINE – ALBERT BRIGGS in large smudged letters.

Which left one bunk for Jonny. The top one, the smooth uncluttered one.

He looked up at it. Secretly he would have preferred the bottom bunk. It would have been more like a cave . . . A bit darker and more secret – with a roof. But there again, what if Albert started to jump about on the top one, or swoop from it on to the floor? And Jonny began to hope *he* wouldn't dive from it himself by accident in the night.

He climbed the steps of the small ladder and peered at the top bunk. No, there was definitely no

sign of a heap of belongings telling him it was his. There wasn't a sign of his stuff anywhere. Very strange . . . his heart began to thump a bit. Don't say there was some other awful plan afoot – like making him go and sleep in the same room as the girls because he hadn't many belongings or posh clothes and didn't need as much space!

Then, as he turned from the ladder and looked across at the window and saw all the chimney pots so close – and the distant Boro football-ground lights on their tall metal frames in the sky – he glimpsed something else. . . . It wasn't quite the same as the one downstairs . . . it was a bit hidden in the corner next to the trunk. It was smaller and made of an old grey blanket. But the same dried-up cabbage leaves were still on top and the cardboard boxes were at the sides.

He jumped down the ladder. Yes – the blue skull was inside, next to all his belongings! And on the newspaper floor was a card saying: JONNY BRIGGS – HIS CAVE in Humph's writing. ". . . which means it can stay there for ever and ever," breathed Jonny in delight.

Quickly he bent down and crawled inside. He sat looking out at the wonderful new bunks, then, taking off his gold belt he put it carefully on a pile of curly-edged comics and crawled out again, ready to start his new and exciting life.

Jonny Briggs was up early for school on Monday morning. He hadn't fallen out of the bunk once, and he quite liked being at the top looking at the cracks in the ceiling. They looked like streams on a map, and he pretended he was an explorer in Stone Age times. That spider in the corner was a huge lion in its lair, and the black heat mark made by the electric light bulb was a forest clearing where the fire was kept burning to keep away wild animals.

Yes . . . having his own bunk made him feel as if he ruled the whole world . . . he heard the snoring roars of the wild animals in the valleys below . . . the black-haired zebra in the bunk bed beneath and the kindly giant gorilla lying on a wooden branch in the distant woods.

The plastic bucket full of pebbles was heavy as Jonny reached the school gates. He looked round to see if Pam had arrived with her bucket of shells, but the only people in sight, complete with their usual skipping-rope, were the twins.

Hastily Jonny humped his bucket away from the twins towards the doors leading to the cloakrooms.

"I'll be right out of their way," he thought. "And besides, even I know that no one's allowed to play about round those school bins. Trust *them* to be there."

But in seconds he was trapped as the twins whipped the rope away and raced across. "What you got there – pie face? Your mam's old scrubbing bucket? Where've you pinched those, out of the park?"

"They're pebbles from Saltburn beach," he muttered.

"If *everybody* pinched pebbles from Saltburn beach there'd be none left," said Josie triumphantly.

"If everybody pinched crayons and glass alleys like you there'd be none left in the *world*," he said — trying not to let his eager leg jerk into a sharp kick as his temper rose. "How could anyone . . ." he thought, "anyone who wanted to make a really good . . . a special giant cave . . . do a thing with those mopheads tormenting them?"

Jinny bent forward, her round rosy cheeks glowing with persistent mischief as she picked up a large pebble – big as a bread bun – and threw it across the school yard so that it spun and slid on the smooth grey ground as, like quick-silver, Jonny ran to fetch it realising – alas, too late – that it was the daftest thing he'd done yet, as Josie smartly tipped the rest of the pebbles out of the bucket and scuttled away, leaving all the rest of the people who were now in the yard to crowd round excitedly – picking up the pebbles and tossing them about while Jonny ran round like a mad thing – hither and thither, hotter and hotter, angrier and angrier – trying to get them all back.

Then, just as he was getting them all back at last, someone actually threw one of the stones at him and he heard the shocked voice of Miss Mills saying sharply: "Who threw that stone?" And by her side, hanging on her arms like little wide-eyed angels and watching it all were those twins!

There was silence in the yard now as some people crept closer to find out what was happening and others moved well away to keep out of trouble.

Then a small thin girl, in a yellow pinafore dress, who was usually as quiet as a mouse, squeaked: "Please miss – I meant to throw it in the bucket . . ." Then she hung her head in shame.

A murmur of relief welled up round Jonny, and his friend Peter smiled happily – while the Brown brothers began to do pop-eyed, gob-gawpy faces at the twins because everyone knew now who'd started it all.

Miss Mills frowned slightly at Jonny, and her mouth began to set in a small hard determined line – just like Miss Broom's mouth. He felt almost near to tears. He just didn't want things to be as bad with Miss Mills as they so often were with Miss Broom. Why should he always get the frowns? None of it was his fault. All he'd done was bring the pebbles to school to make the cave – just like Miss Mills wanted.

Then, to cap it all he heard the loud familiar voice of Mr Badger. He had his early-morning look. His face was all crumpled looking.

"What's going on *now*," he said irritably. "No sooner are some of you in this school playground than it's trouble with a capital T. I'm just fed up with it! Do you understand? Who's to blame this time, Miss Mills?" His eyes bored into Jonny like an electric drill. Jonny stood there staring stolidly at Mr Badger's tweed jacket – hoping to find some sort of help radiating from the little blue flecks in it.

"I think it was an accident," said Miss Mills hastily as she too looked up at Mr Badger.

"It always is," remarked Mr Badger dryly. "And somehow there's always one of the Briggs family involved. There always has been – ever since I began at this school." Then he said, glaring at Jonny, "Tell

me lad, are you *still* the youngest in your family?"

"Yes, sir. I'm the last one, mam said."

"Thank heavens for that . . ." muttered Mr Badger striding away banging his brief-case angrily against his long legs.

"Whatever's been happening, Jonny?" asked Pam when she arrived carrying the bucket of shells.

"Nothing," Jonny gulped in frustration and misery. "Only what you might expect. Only *those two* at it again. How can we build a cave with *them* being part of it all?" He stared sadly at Pam. She looked all neat and calm and she was wearing a dress with a frilled lace collar.

"We'll have to think of something," she said. "We'll just have to find a way, Jonny – like Nana told us."

He began to cheer up, and by the time they'd reached the classroom he was his old normal self and quite fit enough to tie the arms of Josie's green woolly cardigan into knots when no one was looking and sprinkle Jinny's desk top with bits of dusty, smeary, black pencil sharpenings out of the waste-paper basket. Pam found an old picture postcard with a cat on it and wrote *YOU* on the back of it and slipped it in Josie's desk, then stuffed Jinny's pencil case with crumpled-up toffee papers and an apple core while Jinny was reading to Miss Mills, and Josie was away in the toilets.

"Please miss . . ." burst out Jinny when she found out, "Please miss . . . Jonny Briggs and Pamela Dean have been . . . I know it was them, miss . . . they're always doing mean tricks . . . Miss Broom would have sent them straight to Mr Badger if she'd been here . . ."

"You do mean things too . . ." yelled Nadine who was normally very quiet and polite. "You do more mean things than them . . ."

"Be quiet!" shouted Miss Mills, rapping her table with a ruler. "I'm not in the least bit interested in *mean* things. Right now I'm interested in us all building our Giant Cave. And that includes you, Jinny, and you, Josie, and Jonny Briggs *and* Pamela Dean. It means every single person in this classroom

will have to help in some sort of way. So let's get on with it, shall we?"

Immediately all the scuffling and tale-telling subsided and there was an excited silence.

"I shall divide you up into five groups, with a leader. These five leaders will each choose who they want to work in their group. Anyone left over will be able to be in *my* special group. These are the leaders: Jinny, Josie, Peter, Jonny, and Pam. Of course, the leaders will not be able to choose other leaders to be in their groups."

Everyone laughed and they all waited to be chosen.

"The Brown brothers," said Peter, straight away.
"And Nadine, and Lily Spencer and Lionel Watkinson."

Jonny sighed inwardly. It made it a bit harder
having to choose when Peter had got all the good
ones, the ones who were friends.

"You to choose next, Pam," said Miss Mills. Pam hesitated, then because she was interested in sticking the shells on the cave, she chose all the very neat people who'd do it properly and not just throw the shells about and get fed up – or else get them stuck on everything *except* the cave. "I'll have Robin Brooks, and Karen, and Emmy Smith, John and Pauline." She felt quite pleased, and smiled at Jonny. But Jonny was still suspicious. He just couldn't rest until he knew who the twins were going to choose.

"Josie next," smiled Miss Mills.

Josie beamed back like a happy sunflower, then said: "Martin Canebender . . ." and gave Jonny a swift sly glance.

Martin Canebender. Jonny groaned. He was the one person he'd wanted in his lot. Martin Canebender was the biggest boy in the class. He was sometimes in almost as much trouble as Jonny himself. And he was always sitting on things and squashing them by accident – the sort of person it was essential to have on your side. . . . So if Josie had collared Martin Canebender the others in her lot didn't really matter, did they?

"Martin, then Jasmine, Linda and Debby," said Josie quickly.

Miss Mills nodded. "And now you, Jinny," she said.

Jonny held his breath hoping she would choose all the quiet well-behaved people who were left – but instead he heard: "Arrominta Merryweather!"

He nearly sank through the floor in desperation! Arrominta Merryweather was known to everyone in the class as The Human Wall. People always hid behind her or used her to sit at one end of a see-saw while five people sat at the other end. She wasn't particularly fat, but she weighed a ton. Her dad was a weight-lifter.

If she was on your side it was a good thing. But if she wasn't. . . . Jonny shivered.

Jinny smiled innocently at Jonny, then said: "I only need Arrominta to help me with my bit of the cave, Miss Mills. She'll be enough."

Miss Mills looked puzzled, then said: "You'd better take Brian too, Jinny. He's good at building things. And Helen, she always has some good ideas."

Which left four people for Jonny Briggs's lot. Four of the quietest, most well-behaved, polite people in the class who'd never caused trouble in their lives and believed in peace above all else and who'd give in completely if they were sat on or wedged in a corner.

He looked at them sadly and called out their names in a voice which meant *the twins have nearly beaten me but not quite,* . . . as Lesley, Tina, Richard and Scott began to walk across to his corner of the room.

Then they all began to make plans to build the Giant Cave.

5
The Great Exhibition

Jonny Briggs's lot were discussing the pebbles. They were sitting at the back of the classroom in a corner, all relaxed and comfortable. Miss Mills had worked it out so that there was only one group at a time working on the Giant Cave, but she saw to it that they all did a bit of every part: a bit of building up the frame, a bit of painting and moulding the rocks out of cardboard and newspaper, a bit of the outside, a bit of the inside.

Everything was perfect peace. And now, as the huge cave stretched high up towards the ceiling and the Brown brothers perched on the ladders which Mr Box had lent them, it seemed that Jonny Briggs and Pam need never have worried about the twins at all. For the shells were all stuck on in beautiful patterns. Not a single hole was poked through the rather frail walls of the cave.

All that remained now was to finish off the inside fit for a Stone-Age family with pebbles scattered on the floor outside the entrance.

And then – just as Jonny and his group had decided the way they were going to spread those pebbles – Jonny heard the piping voice of Jinny say: "Please miss, I think the cave's good as it is. Pebbles

outside would spoil it, miss. It doesn't need big clumsy pebbles at the door cluttering it up."

Then Josie chipped in and said: "It's stupid having pebbles, miss. Every time you came out of the cave you'd crawl on them and hurt your knees."

Jonny's ears began to go pink with anger. He stopped being relaxed and comfortable. He went all tense and still and his voice went all hoarse and crackly with the upset as he said: "But supposing there was *mud* there, miss? Pebbles would stop it being muddy and all churned up when it rained."

Jonny's lot looked at each other in dismay. Don't say their pebbles were going to get left out after all the other work they'd done! Their pebbles were to be the final finishing touch to the whole project . . . lying neatly in front, all those smooth, rounded, blue-grey stones . . . all restful and at peace. . . .

"We all agree with Jonny," said Pam. "The shells and the stones go together. Shells and pebbles make it look really good." And she stretched out her tongue slowly pretending to lick her cheek but really giving it a rude waggle towards the twins.

"We think *sawdust* would be *far* better on the ground," said Jinny, squeezing up her nose as she glanced in Pam's direction. "Arrominta's got a big bag of sawdust in the cloakroom from when they sweep the floors at the timber yard. We could spread it *everywhere*."

"That is just what we *don't* want, Jinny!" said Miss Mills sharply.

There was a sulky silence, then Josie chirped: "I think we should use the wood that Martin Canebender found on the waste ground behind the shops. We could leave all that lying about instead of pebbles, so that we could pretend we were looking for wood to light a fire and find it all just outside the cave – like in real life. . . ."

"That wood was banned from the start," shouted Jonny indignantly. "It's full of rusty nails, and you know it. Miss Mills says they didn't have *metal* nails in the *Stone* Age." And he pulled a face as well.

"They didn't have paper or cardboard either, stupid," said Josie. "It's only pretending."

Then something happened that was the worst thing possible as far as the cave itself was concerned – because just as Miss Mills was soothing everyone down and saying how well they'd all worked together and that the pebbles would be perfect – the classroom door opened. In walked Miss Broom with a man nobody had seen before. He had horn-rimmed glasses and trousers with very sharp creases up the fronts, and he was carrying a notebook and pencil.

"This is Mr Pickover," Jonny heard Miss Broom say as Miss Mills shook hands with him. "He's come to see how we're all getting on."

All three of them stood and smiled at the Giant Cave and Mr Pickover asked Jonny's class some questions about Stone-Age life. Then he strolled to the back of the classroom and balanced himself on a small chair quite close to Jonny.

"And who's going to go and live in this cave then, and be the family?" he said cheerfully.

In a flash the damage was done.

"Please sir – we are!" called the twins eagerly, their faces alight with bright, winning smiles.

"What charming and enthusiastic pupils you have, Miss Mills." Jonny saw him mark a big tick in his notebook. "Carry on then, young ladies."

"Carry on," is right, thought Jonny grimly as he saw the twins scramble eagerly into the cave and grin at everybody. Trust them to be first in when he was the first person to even try making a cave at all!

The twins peeped out like a couple of gentle little pixies at Mr Pickover and called: "Please sir, can we have a father in, and some children?"

"Certainly you can," smiled Mr Pickover, marking yet another tick in his notebook.

"We'll have Martin Canebender," said Jinny, "and Arrominta Merryweather."

"Please sir, can we have animals as well . . . like a big angry tamed wolf to guard us?"

"You certainly can," Mr Pickover's kindly pink face went even pinker. "What a responsive little group they are, Miss Broom. You ladies seem to be working wonders."

"We'll have Jonny Briggs as the tame wolf sitting outside on some *pebbles*," said Josie, and her voice rang out in triumph.

There was a sudden shiver round the class and a bit of a gasp. They all knew what *that* meant. . . . It was a Declaration of War! Even Miss Mills looked visibly shocked, and gave Miss Broom a quick look.

But Mr Pickover just smiled and put yet another huge tick in his book as he gazed happily at everyone.

"Come along then, Jonny," said Miss Broom at last when nothing happened, as she and Miss Mills stood by the classroom door looking rather nervous.

Jonny felt himself going red and white like a piece of striped seaside rock. Him? Go out there and grovel in front of those twins . . .? In front of the whole class . . .? In front of all his friends? Pretending to be *their* tame wolf? Him go out there and do *that?*

"Er – please miss, I can't miss," he muttered.

"Can't? Why can't you?"

"I just can't, miss," said Jonny miserably, as he looked about him in desperation feeling almost like a trapped wolf at this very moment! "My legs won't move, miss. I think they've gone to sleep." (Which was true – they'd gone all pins and needles.)

Miss Broom looked at Miss Mills. Then they both looked towards Mr Pickover anxiously: "Er – could we have a word with you please Mr Pickover?"

"Yes, yes of course," smiled Mr Pickover, and he jumped up from the small chair and went towards the classroom door: "I've enjoyed visiting this class very much, Miss Broom. I only wish there were more. . . ." Their voices faded as Miss Mills quickly opened the door and Miss Broom edged Mr Pickover out of the classroom and into the corridor. In fact – to Jonny's eyes it seemed as if they almost *pushed* him! Then he saw the three of them drift away down the corridor with Miss Mills and Miss Broom talking ten to the dozen.

In seconds, there was pandemonium!

In seconds, Jonny and the Brown brothers and Pam and Lily Spencer all began to try and get the twins out of the cave. The twins were clutching and

clinging to anything they could find to stop themselves from being dragged from their family seat . . .
which meant hanging on like mad to Arrominta the
Human Wall, and great, big grappling Martin
Canebender. To Jonny it felt like trying to drag
next-door's sharp-clawed tom-cat from inside Razzle's kennel and having a tug-o'-war with a raging
octopus – all rolled into one. The cave swayed and
wobbled about and people began to give little
screams and squeaks and yells (but not too loud as
they were all secretly enjoying it).

85

Then at last there was a great ripping sound as Arrominta's ten-ton body toppled backwards and she sat – *plonk* – on top of Jinny, pushing Josie right through the cardboard side of the cave.

By now there was nothing to be seen but one great big sprawling mass of paper, cardboard, bits of shells, goatskin rug and dried grass, moving about like a giant football full of arms and legs and uproar. Then Miss Broom and Miss Mills rushed back into the classroom.

"Silence!" thundered Miss Broom. "Stay where you are – *everyone!*"

Everyone obeyed immediately – except for Lily Spencer who was in mid-air in the middle of the heap at the time, and landed down to earth with a sharp bang in the silence of the now horror-stricken class.

"Josie – STAND UP!"

Josie stood up shame-facedly and removed a large piece of brown paper from her head.

"Martin Canebender, why are you holding that huge ham-bone? Put it down this minute!"

Martin dropped the large, white well-boiled ham-bone to the floor, and Jonny gave a deep breath of relief.

"Go back to your seats – all of you!"

Masses of untanglings and brushings down began as everyone extricated themselves and sat down meekly. The class sat there surveying what appeared to be a large mountain of rubbish accidentally left behind by the bin-men. Some of the class were almost near to tears, for most of them had worked very hard to make the cave. And now . . . this. . . .

"I hope you're all feeling extremely *proud* of yourselves," said Miss Broom sarcastically. Then she nodded wisely towards Miss Mills and stamped out.

"What on earth happened?" said Miss Mills quietly, after a few more moments' complete silence. "I thought you enjoyed making the cave?"

There was silence again.

Jonny felt his heart beating rapidly. It was all so unfair! If those twins hadn't. . . . Should he stand up right now and tell her? Tell her it was because the twins had deliberately goaded him when that man with the notebook was there . . . Yes. He half stood up – putting up his hand: "P – please M . . ."

But he was too late.

"We were attacked, Miss Mills," said Josie, with a big crocodile sob. "I can feel seven bruises all over my body. My dad'll be sending a letter to Mr Badger."

"And I was *squashed*, miss," said Josie. "And I'd just had three helpings of jam sponge pudding and custard for dinner and it all seemed to squelch inside me. . . ."

"It was your own fault," called Pam. "You lot started it. You've tried to get rid of me and Jonny Briggs ever since that cave started."

"We *never*."

"Yes you *did*."

"That will *do*," said Miss Mills, beginning to look really angry. "Well, unfortunately for all the people concerned, there will have to be a punishment for all this. I shall not ask you to clear it all up now –

because we have some more school work to get through and it wouldn't be fair to the others. Instead, I shall ask Mr Box to leave the cave exactly as it is until tomorrow morning, and Josie, Jinny, Arrominta, Martin, the Brown Brothers, Lily, Jonny and Pamela can all stay behind and tidy it up. You will all *stay behind* while the rest of us are at the Caves Exhibition in the crypt at Middlesbrough Town Hall in the morning. It was meant to be a nice surprise for all of you after your hard work. Now the people I've just mentioned will not be going. I shall tell Mr Badger and Miss Broom why you are staying behind."

An exhibition in the town hall crypt? Jonny groaned. There was nothing better than a good exhibition in the town hall crypt. Once, when Humph was a very little boy, mam had taken him and Rita to a "Dr Who" exhibition there. It was just the sort of place for CAVES. It was all dark and stony looking and mysterious, with heavy doors and stone steps everywhere. Trust him to miss it . . . because of *them*. He scowled at Josie and Jinny and they put their noses in the air and turned away.

It was even worse when Miss Mills started to tell all the others what the exhibition would be like, and how there would be passages to find your way through . . . like an underground maze, and how there were life-sized caves showing stalactites and stalagmites – which looked a bit like stone icicles that grew down from the ceilings and up from the ground.

And there would be caves showing cave drawings, and caves with streams of water running through. And at home-time everyone in the class was talking excitedly about the great Caves Exhibition – everyone except the ones in disgrace.

On the way home from school that night Pam said to Jonny: "Never mind, Jonny. At least you made a cave of your own at home . . . and at least we got the shells and things. And at least we did see it all finished except for the pebbles. And – I think that Miss Mills knew that the twins were really to blame, but she just had to try and be fair. . . ."

"But it wasn't fair," said Jonny. "I've a good mind not to help them to clear up tomorrow. Imagine *helping* them. . . ." He shivered in the sunshine.

"We'll just *have* to, Jonny. We just mustn't get into any more trouble or Mr Badger'll start to get his slipper out, and think how the twins would like that! What we must do is to be *extra* good and not let them get at us at all. That'll make them *really* mad."

That night, at home in his new bunk, Jonny lay there thinking about the school cave. Then he looked at his own little one still there in its corner of his bedroom with the cabbage leaves going all yellow and blotchy on top. "At least *I* can build a proper cave any time I want to," he muttered to himself. Then, because he really felt very happy lying in the strong smell of his new mattress with no toe-nails digging into him, he fell asleep.

It was one of those calm, ordinary days next morning. And on the way to school it was a bit dusty and dull with nothing to look forward to.

After Miss Mills had marked the register it seemed even duller when most of the class hurried off excitedly to the Caves Exhibition at the Town Hall with Miss Mills and Mr Hobbs. Jonny Briggs and company sat mournfully in the classroom listening to a very stern Miss Broom.

"I shall come back to this classroom at play-time," said Miss Broom, "and I shall expect all traces of this disaster to have been neatly disposed of, and all the buckets, brushes and shovels to have been returned to Mr Box. I shall expect to see you all sitting here quietly at your desks getting on with your written work. And if there is the slightest whisper of trouble – off to Mr Badger you go!"

Then Miss Broom left them all to get on with it.

Silently, they stared at each other until Pam whispered to Jonny: "Come on then. Let's get it over with. Help me clear all these bits of paper away."

Quickly they all began to join in.

All . . .?

When the clearing up was finished and they were sitting there quietly getting on with their written work, one of the Brown brothers said: "What happened to Jinny and Josie? They never came back after taking that first cardboard box."

Even Jonny didn't answer this time. He was fed up with the very thought of those twins. All he wanted now was for things to get back to normal again instead of always being in trouble. It wasn't as if he *liked* being in trouble.

So they all sat there, quietly – the classroom all neat now – as they worked away without even a teacher in sight.

Then an amazing thing happened.

Mr Pickover suddenly popped into the classroom in his trousers with the sharp creases and his notebook and pen.

"Hello there!" he said cheerfully. "What a well-disciplined group of children you are, working away all on your own . . . well-behaved . . .quiet . . . amazing! I really called back to see your cave again," he added, "and to see if some of you would like to build a cave for our schools exhibition at Stockton next month. . . . I expect you had to dismantle it to make room for your next project."

"It got a bit battered," mumbled Jonny, by way of explanation.

"They do . . . they do . . ." agreed Mr Pickover. "But they're quite easy to build again aren't they – with busy little workers like you?"

They all nodded. They were too speechless with shock to do anything else.

Then he said: "Well then . . . I'll just write down all your names . . . Miss Broom's class isn't it? Just the right number of people for building this cave at Stockton great schools exhibition. Not too many and not too few, and a good mixture of shapes, sizes and ideas . . ." Then he said – writing their names in his notebook – "I'll tell Mr Badger I've roped you in. Good-bye." And off he went.

When he'd gone, Jonny said, "Phew . . . *us*. The best cave builders for our school in the great schools exhibition at Stockton! Phew!" Then he said doubtfully: "But supposing Mr Badger says . . .?"

But Mr Badger didn't say anything. He was absolutely delighted. He thought it was an honour.

But two people *did* say a lot of things. "It's not fair!" they whined. *"We* should have been chosen too. We only cleared one box because we both had stomach-ache and had to go to the toilet . . . we'll get even with you Jonny Briggs."

But they never did. Not that time anyway.

"Fancy our Jonny actually helping to build *that!*" said mam to dad as they walked round the great schools exhibition at Stockton, a month later. "The things that boy can *do*. I just never would have believed it!"

Dad squeezed her hand. "I'd have believed it," he said. "And maybe one day he'll even build a *house* – never mind a cave."

And they both smiled happily.